THE EARTH DRAGON AWAKES

THE TRAITOR (1885)

DRAGONWINGS (1903)
A *Newbery Honor Book*

THE RED WARRIOR (1939)
Coming soon

CHILD OF THE OWL (1965)

SEA GLASS (1970)

THIEF OF HEARTS (1995)

Dragon of the Lost Sea Fantasies
DRAGON OF THE LOST SEA

DRAGON STEEL

DRAGON CAULDRON

DRAGON WAR

Chinatown Mysteries
THE CASE OF THE GOBLIN PEARLS

THE CASE OF THE FIRECRACKERS

Edited by Laurence Yep
AMERICAN DRAGONS
Twenty-Five Asian American Voices

Awards
Laura Ingalls Wilder Award

THE EARTH DRAGON AWAKES

The San Francisco Earthquake of 1906

Laurence Yep

■ HarperCollins*Publishers*

Photos on pp. 115 (top) and 116 (top) courtesy of the Museum of the City of San Francisco.
Photos on pp. 115 (bottom), 116 (bottom), and 117 courtesy of the Bancroft Library,
University of California, Berkeley.

Library of Congress Cataloging-in-Publication Data
Yep, Laurence.
The earth dragon awakes : the San Francisco earthquake of 1906 /
Laurence Yep.— 1st ed.
p. cm.
Summary: Eight-year-old Henry and nine-year-old Chin love to read
about heroes in popular "penny dreadful" novels, until they both experience
real courage while trying to survive the 1906 San Francisco earthquake.
ISBN-10: 0-06-027524-3 (trade bdg.) — ISBN-13: 978-0-06-027524-2
(trade bdg.)
ISBN-10: 0-06-027525-1 (lib. bdg.) — ISBN-13: 978-0-06-027525-9
(lib. bdg.)
1. Earthquakes—California—San Francisco—Juvenile fiction.
[1. Earthquakes—California—San Francisco—Fiction. 2. San Francisco
(Calif.)—History—20th century—Fiction. 3. Courage—Fiction.
4. Survival—Fiction. 5. Chinese Americans—California—San Francisco—
Fiction.] I. Title.
PZ7.Y44Ear 2006   2005017665
[Fic]—dc22   CIP
                              -                           AC

Typography by Larissa Lawrynenko
1 2 3 4 5 6 7 8 9 10
❖
First Edition

To Ellen and Russell Coile,
who are more than prepared for
the next Big One

PREFACE

The characters are imaginary. However, the events in the novel are based on fact. I could not have made up so many grand and terrible things.

IT IS EARLY EVENING in San Francisco. Streetlights come on. People hurry home. No one knows about the danger below.

Underneath their feet, the earth begins to stir.

AT THAT MOMENT, the Travis family is too busy to worry. Henry's parents are going to the opera.

Henry's mother calls from upstairs, "Ah Sing, have you seen my silk shawl?"

Mr. Travis bellows, "Ah Sing, I need a new shirt. You've shrunk another one."

Mrs. Travis pats her husband's belly affectionately. "Don't blame Ah Sing, dear. It's time for a diet."

"I am not fat," Mr. Travis protests. "My stomach is as solid as the earth." His belly shows through the open hole on his shirt. It jiggles when he moves. "It's all Ah Sing's fault. He does something to my shirts. And that's why I keep losing buttons."

2

"Don't change shirts, dear," Mrs. Travis says. "We don't have time. Mr. Caruso will be so disappointed if you show up late for his Don José."

"I would rather go to the roller-skating carnival," Mr. Travis grumbles. "They're giving out a thousand-dollar prize for the best costume."

"I wish we could go roller-skating, too," says Henry. He was eager to try out his new skates. He'd gotten them for Easter two days before.

"We'll have a picnic next Sunday," Mrs. Travis suggests.

"Enrico Caruso should be grateful if I don't go tonight." Mr. Travis yawns. "I'm so tired from work. I'll just nap there. Even his bellowing won't keep me awake."

"If his singing doesn't, my elbow will," teases Mrs. Travis. "I had Ah Sing sharpen it today." She jabs him in the side.

Mr. Travis rubs his ribs. "That's why I need padding there."

"Maybe I could go to the skating carnival with Ah Sing," Henry says hopefully.

"I know you're dying to try your new skates," his mother says, "but the carnival's not for children."

Ah Sing and his son, Chin, come upstairs. Ah Sing is the Travises' houseboy. He cleans and cooks and helps around the house.

3

Chin has the cloak. Ah Sing has the sewing basket.

"Henry, help Ah Sing find the button," Mr. Travis orders.

Ah Sing has helped Mr. Travis get ready many times. "I got plenty," Ah Sing says. "I sweep. I find. I keep." From his pocket, he takes out a matching button. On his coat, he has stuck a needle with thread. It is the right color.

Ah Sing is like the captain of a ship in a storm. He tells Henry and Chin to hold Mr. Travis's shirt closed while he sews the button on.

Henry winks at Chin. Chin is nine and Henry is eight. They have become good friends. Though Chin has been in America for only two years, he already speaks English better than his father.

Suddenly Henry's pet dog, Sawyer, begins to howl.

Mr. Travis scrunches up his face. "You should take Sawyer. He can sing with Caruso."

"He's been doing that all day. I don't know what's wrong with him. We took him to the vet," Mrs. Travis says. "He's perfectly healthy."

Henry puts his dog in his room. Then he returns to help his parents some more. He fetches his mother's beaded purse. His father misplaces his top hat twice. Both times, Henry finds it.

Ah Sing, Chin and Henry manage to steer them to the

front door. Mrs. Travis stops on the threshold. She picks an umbrella that matches her gown.

"There isn't a rain cloud in the sky," protests Mr. Travis.

"You never know when an umbrella will come in handy," his wife says calmly.

By the doorway, they have not one but two umbrella stands. They are filled with umbrellas.

"You have too many choices," Mr. Travis teases. "If your collection were smaller, it wouldn't take so long to pick one."

"If you didn't lose them, I wouldn't need so many," Mrs. Travis says. She finally selects two.

Somehow Ah Sing, Chin and Henry get them on their way.

Ah Sing begins to pick up the discarded shawls, capes and cloaks from the floor. He tells the boys to do their schoolwork.

Henry is on Easter vacation, but he has homework. Chin does not attend American school yet, but he hopes to go soon. At the moment, he goes to Chinese school in Chinatown. Because Chinese school does not celebrate Easter, he would normally have gone tonight. However, the Travises had asked Ah Sing and Chin to watch Henry.

Sawyer crouches in a corner of Henry's bedroom. He is terrified. Henry makes a place for Sawyer on his bed. Then, looking out the window, Henry begins his art assignment. He has to draw his neighborhood.

Chin lies on the floor and starts his essay about his home in China. He has almost too much to write. The Americans make it difficult for a Chinese man to bring his family to America. It has been hard enough for just Chin to come. He had to study for months and months before he got on the boat to America. He needed to know everything. He had to memorize every house in his village, every field, every window, every tree, every animal.

The immigration officials spent a week asking him questions. If he had made a mistake, they would have assumed he was lying. They would have sent him back to China. They would have sent his father back, too.

Chin would have liked to go home. But his father's salary is very important. An American dollar is worth so much more in China. Chin's father can support his mother, his grandparents and several other relatives.

Henry finishes his picture quickly. The wooden houses press against one another. They are all three stories high. The front doors are all one story from the ground. The houses all have bay windows. Except for the paint, they all look the same.

Sawyer whimpers. Henry tries to pet him. He can feel his dog shivering. "What's spooked you, boy?" He does not want to move and disturb Sawyer more. So he tells Chin to open his schoolbag and get his present.

Chin makes sure Ah Sing is downstairs. Then he sneaks a flimsy paper book from his schoolbag. On the cover, a cowboy blazes away with a six-gun as another cowboy falls to the dust. The whole day, Chin has been looking forward to this.

None of their parents approve of the cheap books. Henry's mother even calls them "penny dreadfuls." All the boys at Henry's school like them and pass them around. Henry has been helping Chin learn English by reading the dreadfuls with him.

"When I grow up, I'm going to be a lawman just like Marshal Earp." Henry pretends to blaze away with his six-shooters. "I'm never going to be like my father. All he does is add up numbers all day in that old bank."

"And my father washes dishes," Chin sighs.

"Neither is exciting," Henry agrees.

Sawyer lifts his head and begins to howl again. As he tries to calm his dog again, Henry wishes he knew what was upsetting him. Everything else seems so peaceful. And boring. Just like his parents.

Henry is puzzled, but he promises, "Don't worry, boy. I won't let anything happen to you."

Late evening
Tuesday, April 17, 1906
Deep beneath San Francisco

M R. TRAVIS IS WRONG. The earth is not solid.

Deep in the center of the earth, it is very hot. It is so hot that even rock melts.

To us, the land and oceans seem huge. But they are only the surface of our world.

Compared to the earth's core, the surface is very thin. It floats on the hot core like a piecrust.

The surface itself is broken into pieces called plates. Each bit of land and sea is on some plate. Tall mountains and deep seafloors, people, animals, fish and forests are all on top of these plates.

San Francisco is on the edge of the North American Plate. Next to it is the Pacific Plate, which holds the Pacific

Ocean. The Pacific Plate moves two inches to the north-west every year. That seems slow to us. Your fingernails grow that much in twelve months.

The two plates shove each other like two wrestlers. The place where they meet is called the San Andreas Fault. It stretches for 650 miles from the southwest to the northeast and reaches 10 miles wide in some places. Many other smaller cracks branch from it like twigs from a tree.

The two plates bump and grind against each other all the time. Usually no one feels it. But sometimes they shove very hard. We call those earthquakes.

Over the years the earth has moved many times under San Francisco. But it has been thirty-eight years since the last strong earthquake.

People have forgotten how bad they can be.

But they will soon remember.

CHIN AND HENRY are sup-
posed to sleep. Instead they read by the
light of the streetlamps. They are still reading when Henry's parents come home. Mr.
Travis has managed to lose yet another
umbrella.

Mrs. Travis gives Chin a piece of candy
before he leaves the house. "Don't let Mr. Travis know I
gave this to you," she says with a wink. "Or he'll turn the
house upside down to find my secret hoard."

Ah Sing and Chin leave the Travis house. As they wait
for the cable car, Chin eats Mrs. Travis's candy. He thinks
about his own mother.

"Do you think Mother misses us?" he asks his father.

"Every day," his father says.

Chin will have to spend most of his life here, like his father. Will Chin forget his mother after a while?

"Do you miss Mother?" he asks his father.

"Every day," his father says.

It seems forever before the cable car comes. Chin can feel the book hidden under his shirt. He can't wait to get back to it. When he reads, he forgets his boredom. He forgets his loneliness.

When the cable car finally arrives, sleepy Chinese climb down. Like Ah Sing and Chin, they work in the houses. They also live in them. But tonight, on their night off, they have gone into Chinatown. Ah Sing and Chin could have stayed with the Travises, too. But Ah Sing insists they live in Chinatown. He doesn't want Chin to forget he's Chinese.

Their fellow houseboys fuss over Chin. He reminds them of the children they left behind in China. He usually welcomes the attention. Tonight, though, he is impatient. He wants to read more of his new book. He climbs quickly onto the cable car.

The crew greets him. They are friends with their Chinese passengers. They even wear silver pins of a dragon. The jewelry is a gift from the houseboys.

The car lurches forward. The cable rattles and hums

in its bed beneath the rails. Like a long metal snake, it wriggles along its track. The gripman hooks the cable car onto it. The cable car hitches a ride on the moving cable.

Silvery tracks lead up and down hills. On the crests, Chin sees San Francisco spread out before them. Streetlamps glitter like jewels.

American houses perch shoulder to shoulder like pigeons. Beyond them rise the tall buildings of the business district. Some of them tower so high that people say they scrape the sky. They call them skyscrapers.

Chin usually enjoys the view. Tonight he only wants the cable car to go faster.

Chin and his father say good-bye to the cable-car crew and get off in Chinatown. It is so much bigger than his village in China. There are around ten thousand Chinese who live here. But not all of them speak the same dialect as he does. Though they come from China, he cannot always understand them.

So it is home and yet not home to Chin. Even the buildings are different. They are all so much taller than the ones in his village. Some are three or even four stories high. A few look like the Chinese ones Chin saw in Hong Kong before he got on the ship to come here. Most are American buildings. They look so plain compared to the ones at home. There are no tiled roofs or carved windows. But the

Chinese have added signs and decorations to them. The American buildings look like they are wearing Chinese disguises.

Though it is late, Chinatown is still very busy. Chinese shop in the stores. They eat in the restaurants. Americans dine with them. Some are ladies in evening dress and gentlemen in top hats. Some are in costume with roller skates draped over their chairs. They have been to the carnival.

Chin can't wait to get back to their room. But his father drags him all over Chinatown on dull errands. He picks up a couple of Chinese newspapers. Then he buys a bag of apples for the Travises. Mrs. Travis hopes she can get Mr. Travis to eat them instead of cake. (Chin has his doubts about that.)

Everywhere they go, Ah Sing bumps into friends. He always stops to chat. Chin follows his father impatiently. Finally they return to their tenement.

As they pass the little temple, their neighbor Ah Quon comes out. He dodges around a wagon and crosses the street to them.

Chin groans silently. Ah Quon means another delay. Worse, he always stinks of blood from his work in his butcher shop. Many people avoid him because of that. He goes to the temple every night. He says he needs all the help he can get. Next to the priests, he prays more than anyone in Chinatown.

Tonight, though, he has been asking heaven to keep the Earth Dragon quiet. The animals in his shop have been frightened.

"If I were a chicken and saw your knife, I'd be scared, too," Ah Sing says.

"But not this way. They're terrified," Ah Quon says. "At home, animals know when there's going to be an earthquake." He scratches his head. "I can't blame the Earth Dragon if he gets upset. There are all these people stomping on his ceiling." He begins to tiptoe.

"The Earth Dragon has shaken the city before," Ah Sing laughs. "We're still holding on to his back."

"Like fleas on a dog." Ah Quon grins nervously. "But what if he gets really mad?"

Ah Sing does not take Ah Quon's fears seriously. He slaps his friend on the back. "We've been through lots of earthquakes here. If you're still alive, you pick up and go on."

Chin thinks about Henry's dog, Sawyer. Silently he asks the Earth Dragon to keep his temper.

Together with Ah Quon, they climb the tenement stairs. When Chin had first seen the tenement, he had thought it was a hollow hill full of caves. It didn't seem very Chinese either.

As they mount the steep steps, Chin hears the clacking of mahjong tiles. In that game, players match pieces. Someone is playing the scales on a fiddle. Other people are arguing. Another person is crying. Still another is laughing. It is a small village in itself.

Sometimes Chin wishes they didn't live on the top floor. It is very tiring to walk up three flights after a long day.

In their room, his father takes an empty box from a neatly stacked column of boxes. "You might as well put your book in here."

"I already have a box for my schoolbooks," Chin says.

"I mean the ones that Mr. Henry gives you," Ah Sing sighs.

Embarrassed, Chin puts the book into the box. "You knew?"

"I can feel your library." Ah Sing rubs his back. "I think I still have dents there." He holds up the mattress. Quickly Chin picks up the books beneath it and places them inside the box.

"You can read them as long as you get good report cards," his father warns.

"I will," Chin promises. He pulls out his book. "May I read one chapter?"

His father sighs. "It's better than having you sneak outside."

"You know I've been reading on the stairs?" Chin asks guiltily.

His father smiles. "I'm interested in everything you do. It just may not seem like it because I'm usually busy."

Chin snuggles up in bed. Soon he loses himself in Marshal Earp's adventures. His father is kind, and he works hard. But he is no hero. No one wants to read about peeling potatoes and washing dishes.

F AR BELOW SAN Francisco, the
Pacific Plate grinds against the North
American Plate. It rubs harder than it ever
has. The two plates slip and twist. Dirt and
rock stir and tumble. In an instant, 375,000
square miles shake violently.

All over the world, there are machines
that measure earthquakes. Their needles start to wag
crazily. In those days, scientists measured earthquakes in a
different way. Today we use the Richter scale. The Great
Earthquake was 8.25 by modern standards.

The surface rips open for almost 290 miles. From Los
Angeles in the south to Oregon in the north and east to
Nevada, cliffs fall into the ocean, hills crumble into valleys,

mountains crack, rivers twist, ancient trees topple and crash.

But San Francisco is at the center of the destruction. It sits on the bull's-eye of a target. In its houses, almost 343,000 people lie sleeping or are just waking.

It is as if more than 18 million sticks of dynamite explode beneath them. That is more force than the atom bomb that struck Hiroshima.

This is the Earthquake of 1906, when the earth shook so terribly.

5:12 A.M.
Wednesday, April 18, 1906
Travis household
Sacramento Street area

S AWYER HAS BEEN restless the whole evening. He whimpers all the time. He keeps waking his master. Henry does not sleep well either.

It is twilight, just before dawn. Sawyer lets out a howl. Henry sits up and tries to calm his pet. "Everything's all right, boy." Around him is the same boring room. The same bureau. The same bookcase. The same desk.

Then he sees the gleam of his new roller skates. They are hanging on the back of a chair. Perhaps not everything is boring. He can hardly wait to go skating.

Suddenly Henry hears a low rumbling. It sounds like a train coming. His books bounce on the shelves as if they're alive. Henry has been through earthquakes before. He is not worried.

The shaking stops for a moment. He takes a breath. The rumbling starts again.

The bookcase tilts back and forth. The books fall. *Thud. Thud. Thud.*

Henry's heavy oak bed hops with them. It skips like a grasshopper. He holds his dog tight.

More books spill out of the bookcase. The chest of drawers dances a jig. The walls groan. The wooden floor ripples like waves of an ocean. Windows rattle. Doors thump in their frames.

The whole house shakes like Sawyer when he has an itch. Plates crash in the kitchen below. Pictures and then plaster drop from the wall. Old boards show through the gaps. Henry coughs in the growing cloud of dust.

And still the shaking goes on. His bed and all his furniture circle in a slow waltz around the room.

Then the window shatters. The shade flies up with a flap. The other houses in the neighborhood jerk about. Immediately across the street, the Smiths' house falls apart. Bricks rain on the ground. Dust rises and hides the street. From within the cloud, Henry hears screams.

His father bangs at his door. "Henry, Henry, are you all right?" he calls from the hallway.

"Yes. How about you and Mama?" Henry asks. He stumbles out of bed. The floor shakes so much that he cannot stand. He crawls to the door.

"We're fine, darling," his mother says.

Henry tries to open his door, but it won't budge. The door is now crooked in the frame. "It's jammed," he says.

"Don't worry," promises his father. "I'll get you out."

He hears another rumble. There is a crash above him. He dodges when a chunk of ceiling falls. Bricks shower down. They smash against the floor. Boards splinter and break.

CHIN IS POURING water from a pitcher into a bowl. He needs to wash up. Then they will catch a cable car to Henry's house to cook breakfast for the Travises.

Suddenly everything trembles. The bowl creeps across the table. Then even the table crawls away. Chin spills water everywhere.

"You can write your mother about your first earthquake," his father says unworriedly.

The floor rolls under them like a wooden sea. The bowl slips over the edge and crashes. Boxes tumble from the stack. Their possessions scatter across the boards. Chin and his father drop to their knees.

Ah Sing tries to sound brave. "The Earth Dragon must

22

be scratching," he laughs.

Chin tries to be just as fearless. When the room stills, he tries to joke like his father. "He must really have an itch."

Before his father can answer, the trembling begins again.

Chin waits for it to stop. But it goes on and on. The tenement creaks and groans like an old giant. Their bed and bureau prowl like hungry animals.

Ah Sing crawls over. He puts his arms around Chin. "Don't be scared," he says. Ah Sing's voice sounds funny because he is shaking with the room.

Beneath them, unseen timbers crack like sticks. The next instant, one side of the room tilts upward. They slide helplessly with all the furniture toward the opposite wall. Chin feels like a doll. Their belongings crash and thump as they pile up.

His father forces him under the table.

"The tenement is falling!" his father shouts.

Walls crack and crumble. Windows shatter. Broken glass sprays like little daggers.

Chin's stomach feels funny when the room itself drops. They bounce against the floor as it stops with a jerk. For a moment, they lie there. Their neighbors scream from the middle level. Ah Sing and Chin's room is crushing them.

Then the floor twitches. It plunges again. There are more screams. This time it is the ground level that is smashed.

Their floor gives one final thump and stops.

Dazed, Chin peeks out from beneath the table. He sees cracks. They spread like a crazy spiderweb around all the walls. Spurts of powdery plaster puff out. The walls crumble like paper. The ceiling drops down on them.

THE EARTHQUAKE makes the ground bounce up and down, twisting it back and forth like an old towel. Horses bolt into the street from firehouses. On Mission Street, cattle are being herded from the docks to the slaughter yard. They stampede in terror. They trample and gore a man.

One sixth of the city is on landfill. Dirt, rock and debris have been dumped along the shore of the bay and into the creeks and ponds. Homes and apartments and stores have been built on top. Valencia Street was constructed this way.

The earthquake tosses water from deep underground and mixes it with the landfill. The ground stops being solid then. That is called liquefaction. The soil becomes like quicksand and sucks entire houses down. That happens on Valencia Street.

Even on more solid ground, buildings collapse like houses of cards.

Thousands of people are trapped all over the city.

C HIN CANNOT SEE. He cannot move. He can barely breathe.

In the darkness, he hears his father cough. "Are you all right, Chin?"

His father is holding him tight. Chin tries to answer. But dust fills his mouth and throat. So he simply nods. Since his father can't see him, Chin squeezes his arm.

Then he shifts around so he can raise one hand. He can feel the tabletop, but its legs have collapsed. Fallen pieces of ceiling and wall have turned the space into a tiny cave.

His father pushes at the wreckage around him. "It won't budge," he grunts.

Chin shoves with him. "The whole ceiling fell on us."

If his father hadn't pulled him under the table, he would have been crushed.

But now they are buried alive.

Overhead, they hear footsteps.

"The Earth Dragon's mad," a man screeches in fear.

"Here!" cries Ah Sing.

"Help us!" Chin yells, too.

From nearby, someone hollers, "Fire!"

The footsteps run away.

Chin and his father shout until they are hoarse.

No one hears them though.

Trapped under the rubble, they will be buried alive.

"We'll have to rescue ourselves," his father says. "Try to find a loose section." They squirm and wriggle. There is a big slab of plaster near Chin's head. He gropes with his hands until they feel the plaster. Powdery chunks crumble into his hands.

He hears his father digging. Chin claws at the broken boards and plaster. Dust chokes their noses and throats. Still they scrabble away like wild animals.

HENRY COUGHS IN the swirling dust. Chimney bricks lie in heaps around him. A wall has disappeared. He can see right into his parents' bedroom. Or what was their bedroom. It is gone now. So is the big chimney. Most of it toppled into their room. Their floor has given way under the weight and crashed below.

His father pounds at the door. "Henry, are you all right?"

He covers his mouth against the scented dust. All his mother's perfume bottles have broken. The house creaks and groans ominously.

Sawyer yips in fear.

"Help me!" begs Henry.

His father's voice calms him. "We'll get you out, Henry. I'm going to get a crowbar. You dress in the meantime."

Henry obediently puts on his clothes. Though the house is still trembling, dressing gives him something to do. Then he scoops up Sawyer.

Henry clutches his pet. The crowbar scrapes at the doorframe.

With a crack of wood, the door splinters and swings open. Henry sees his father, his nightshirt stuffed into his trousers. His mother stands behind his father. Her usually tidy hair is all tangled. She is wearing her silk shawl over her nightgown.

His father hugs him. "Thank heaven you're all right."

His mother hugs him, too. Then she cleans his face with her shawl. "You're all dusty."

"So are you," Henry laughs with relief.

They look through the hole in the wall. "Yes, that could have been us in the next room," says his father.

"If the chimney had fallen the other way, it could have crushed you," his mother says.

The house rumbles dangerously as they go downstairs. Henry carries Sawyer in his arms. The stairs sway under his feet. He hardly dares to breathe. Their house seems as if it will fall apart at any moment. "Please hold together," he prays silently.

Mr. Travis pauses by the living room. Mrs. Travis gives a cry when she sees it. Grandmother's piano has disappeared under a pile of bricks, board and plaster.

Then she squares her shoulders. "At least we're alive," she says. "That's the important thing."

His father winds the little crank on their telephone on the hallway wall. "Hello, operator. Hello, hello?" he shouts into the mouthpiece. Finally he hangs up the receiver. "The lines must be down."

The front door is jammed, too. His father pries at it with his crowbar.

Sawyer barks from Henry's arms, urging Mr. Travis to hurry.

At last, the door cracks off its hinges. Mr. Travis tugs the door open.

They freeze in the doorway. Across the street, the front of the Smiths' house has crumbled onto the street. However, the rooms are still intact. Trapped on the second floor, the Smiths are stunned. They stand stiffly, like Henry's cousin's dolls in their toy house.

An elderly couple, the Rossis, aren't so lucky. Their frame house down the block has collapsed on top of them.

The whole street has split open. The cable-car tracks have been twisted into strange shapes like shining wire. Some houses tilt at odd angles. They look as if they are peering over someone's shoulder. The pipes under the street have broken. Water gushes out like a fountain.

Henry squeezes his eyes shut. But when he opens them again, the nightmare is still there.

CHIN AND HIS FATHER dig in the darkness. He just hopes they are digging out of the rubble. His arms ache. He is covered with cuts and bruises. Dust chokes his mouth and throat. He feels as if he cannot even breathe. The earth has swallowed them up.

"Fire!" people cry from above. He feels the thumping of running feet.

He screams, "Let me out!"

His father stops digging and wraps his arms around him. "Don't panic!"

But fear twists inside Chin like a snake. He is so dry he cannot even cry. He just lies there. His fingernails are broken. His fingers are bleeding.

They will never escape. He thinks about his mother. She won't know how they died.

Suddenly a breeze brushes his face like a soft hand. He smells fresh air.

He forgets his pain. He forgets he is tired. He scrapes at the wreckage. But he can make only a narrow tunnel. It is barely big enough for him.

"Don't worry about me," urges his father. "Save yourself."

"I'll get help," Chin promises.

"You're the important one," his father says.

Chin crawls up through the passage, leaving his father behind. He would be scared to be left alone in the darkness. Until now he didn't realize how brave his father is. Or how much he loves Chin.

Chin's hands break into the open. They flap frantically like the wings of a scared bird.

"There's someone alive," a man shouts in Chinese.

All Chin can do is croak in answer.

Above him, he hears feet. Someone starts to dig. Boards and bricks and plaster chunks thump to the side. Blindly Chin helps his rescuer widen the hole.

Strong hands grip his wrists. He feels himself rising until he sees Ah Quon's big, grinning face.

"You're the biggest turnip that I ever pulled up," Ah Quon laughs in relief. He hauls Chin onto the rubble.

Chin has only one thought on his mind. "Father," he gasps and points below him.

As Ah Quon digs for his father, Chin manages to spit out the plaster dust. Then he tears at the debris, too.

HENRY'S FATHER organizes the rescuers. First, they find a ladder and get the Smiths out of their home.

Then Mr. Travis leads everyone to the collapsed house. Sawyer jumps from Henry's arms. His dog barks excitedly at one spot. Henry crouches on the rubble. The Rossis' voices sound faint inside the ruins.

Hurriedly the rescuers lift away bricks and boards and plaster. Henry ties Sawyer to an iron fence with a rope. Then he helps his father and mother go through the wreckage.

Everyone freezes when the ground starts to shake again. A brick falls from a nearby building. When the trembling stops, they look around nervously.

Mr. Travis calms everyone. "We don't have time to be scared. There's too much to do." He ignores the danger and starts to dig.

Henry thought that Marshal Earp was brave. But no outlaw was as deadly as Nature. This is an even bigger battle. And his father doesn't back down.

He joins his father. Mrs. Travis is right by him. Soon everyone is digging again.

These are ordinary people Henry sees every day. "They're acting just like heroes," he says to his mother.

Mrs. Travis throws a brick to the side. "You can't judge a book by its cover," she says.

Henry works until his back aches. He stands up for a moment to rest. To the south, a plume of black smoke rises high into the air and then curls like a question mark. "I think there's a fire."

"Don't worry," says his father. "We have the best fire department in the world."

"My house," one of the other neighbors cries. Smoke rises from his house three doors down.

"The firemen will be here soon," Mr. Travis insists. But he sends Mr. Smith to the nearest firehouse. Then he splits the rescuers into groups. Some stay with him to dig through the rubble.

The others form a bucket brigade. Water spills from the

broken water main. That is the big pipe that supplies water to the houses on the street. They fill buckets with water. Then they pass each bucket along to the head of the line, who throws the water on the flames. Another line passes the empty pails back.

The searchers finally find the Rossis under their heavy oak bed. Though it's broken, it has protected them.

"My father cut the tree down and made it himself," Mr. Rossi says. His arm is broken. His wife has a bad cut on her forehead. It bleeds a lot.

Mr. Travis flags down a surrey. He asks the driver of the little carriage to take the couple to the hospital.

"I'm busy," says the driver.

"But they need a doctor," Mr. Travis argues.

"Do I look like a charity?" The driver laughs.

"We'll walk there on our own," Mr. Rossi says and stumbles to his feet. But Mr. Rossi is very old. Henry doubts he will get farther than a block.

"I'll pay you to take them," his father says.

The driver scowls. "Fifty dollars."

"That's robbery!" his father splutters.

The driver shrugs. "I don't know what hospitals are still standing. I might have to drive a long way."

Mr. Travis takes the money from his wallet. It is all he has in there.

They help the Rossis into the surrey and watch them drive away.

"Trouble brings out the worst in some people," grumbles Mr. Travis.

"Trouble brings out the best in people, too," Mrs. Travis adds. She points at the bucket brigade.

CHIN AND HIS FATHER sit on the rubble by the hole. Their home is now a huge garbage heap. Here is a shoe. There a plate.

"Did anyone else get out?" Chin asks.

Ah Quon shrugs. "Not that I know of."

Dust rises in ribbons like tiny ghosts. Their neighbors are gone. The three of them are the only survivors from the building. Why are they the lucky ones? Why did the others die?

Chinatown looks like a broken set of toy blocks. Some buildings tilt threateningly. Others are mounds of rubble like their home. A few blocks away he can see St. Mary's church. The crucifix has fallen from its steeple. Smoke rises from a nearby tenement. More smoke rises from warehouses in the east.

Across the way, the small temple is crowded. Terrified people stand outside. They clasp their hands in prayer and bow their heads. They burn incense sticks and written prayers. The fragrance mixes with the dust and smoke in the air. Some even pray in the street.

Shocked people wander around Chinatown. No one wants to be inside the old, rickety buildings.

A man hurries by with a half dozen empty birdcages. Another man pushes a baby carriage full of flowerpots. A third carries a phonograph. He wears the funnel-shaped speaker on his head like a hat.

The ground starts to shake again. People shout and scream. Within the temple, the praying grows even louder. This earthquake does not last long. But the earlier quakes have weakened many buildings already.

A section of a building smashes into the street. It scatters cobblestones like missiles. One barely misses Chin.

He worries about his friend. "I hope Henry's all right."

"Let's look for a telephone," his father says.

Bells clang. They draw closer by the second.

"Out of the way," a man shouts in English.

A plume of steam rushes toward them. The crowd darts to either side. Suddenly they can see the big horses pulling the fire engine. Their great hooves clop on the cobblestones. A fire captain shouts through a megaphone, "Out of the way!" He waves his hand anxiously. When the wagon slips on the stones, he nearly falls from his seat.

The wagon halts by the burning building. Flames wag out of the windows like salamander tongues.

The firemen leap from the wagon. They unwind the big hose. One of them stands with the hose's nozzle in his hands. He spreads his legs and waits. Another uses a big wrench to open the hydrant. Water spurts out and then stops.

"The water main must be broken," one of them shouts. He sounds both scared and frustrated.

"We'll try the next one," the captain says.

"First, it's falling buildings. Now it's fire," Ah Quon says. "We'd better go to Portsmouth Square. It's an open space. It should be safe."

Ah Sing and Chin get to their feet and join the crowd. The twisted cable-car tracks look like the strokes of a mysterious, dreadful word.*

Piles of brick, wood and stone lie everywhere. However, one store has already opened. The owner hastily changes

*Chinese words are characters based on pictures. Strokes make up each character.

the prices on his signs. He is tripling everything.

A few steps ahead, a heavy sack thumps against the cobblestones. "Hey!" his father yells, jumping to the side with Chin.

"Sorry," a man calls from the second story of a store. "We've got to get our stuff out."

Sacks lie all around. Baskets break when they hit the street. Fruit spills onto the cobblestones.

Things rain down on them from the upper stories. They have to keep dodging. Someone in a stationery store throws out a case. The lid comes open. Red gift envelopes scatter like bright leaves.

In their hurry to save their possessions, people throw everything onto the street. Suitcases. Pots. Woks. Chairs. Clothes.

The newspaper office is deserted. The printers have escaped. They have dropped trays of metal characters. They lie on the floor like glittering rice grains.

They pass by an automobile. The heavy machine rests on its side like a sleeping animal. A little farther on, a wagon has been turned upside down. The horse lies dead in its traces. A stone from a building fell on it.

Chin and his father stop by the building that belongs to their clan. They ask to use the telephone, but the clerk shakes his head. "All the telephone lines are down."

"We can't call Henry then." Chin worries. Does Henry's house still stand? Are the Travises even alive?

"We'll walk to their house when it's safe," his father promises.

They pass by the firemen, who look exasperated as water trickles from the new hydrant.

Ah Quon, Ah Sing and Chin hurry. None of them wants to be trapped in a burning Chinatown.

They reach Portsmouth Square at last. The lawn stretches for an entire city block. This morning, though, Chin cannot see the grass. It is filled with people. There are many Americans as well as Chinese. People walk around in a daze. Others weep.

Across the street to the east, police bustle in and out of the Hall of Justice. The mayor is there, too, because city hall has been wrecked. Seeing the mayor reassures Chin. Things are under control.

Abruptly he hears shouts. The crowd stirs like a flock of startled pigeons. People run by. A man almost knocks Chin over. His father grabs the rude man. "What's the idea?"

The man points, terrified. "There's a bull stampeding." He tears free and runs on.

The bull's bellows draw near.

"What's a bull doing here?" his father wonders.

"They bring cattle in from the boats to the slaughter

yards," explains Ah Quon. "The earthquake could have hit when they were bringing a herd in."

It is already too late to escape.

"Hrunh!"

A huge bull gallops toward them. Its eyes are wide with terror. Its sides glisten with sweat. Its hooves thud against the ground. It lowers its horns. They look wickedly sharp. Ah Quon unrolls his apron and takes out a knife. But the bull dodges and heads for Chin instead.

His father darts in front of the bull. As he flaps his arms, he shouts, "Run, boy."

The bull knocks Ah Sing to the side.

"Father!" Chin cries.

The bull is right in front of him.

Then there is a sharp crack. The bull jerks to a halt. A policeman stands there with a pistol. He takes aim and shoots again. The bull falls on its side.

The policeman approaches the bull cautiously. It lies twitching. Then he eyes Ah Quon's knife suspiciously.

Ah Quon drops the knife and holds his hands up. "Butcher," he says quickly in English. "I butcher."

"Then get cutting," the policeman says, holstering his pistol. "We might as well have steaks."

While Ah Quon sets to work, Chin goes over to his father. "Are you all right?" Chin asks him in Chinese.

His father winces. "It's my ankle."

"You saved me," Chin says. Chin was wrong about his father. He isn't dull at all. He should have his own book, like Marshal Earp.

But he also feels embarrassed. He was wrong to think his father wasn't a hero.

As Ah Sing rests, people pile up the broken crates and furniture. They start fires in the square. They boil water from the broken mains so it will be safe to drink. Soon they are roasting steaks, too.

Several times, the earth shivers, but the tremors never last long. Each time, people pause nervously. They check the buildings surrounding the square. But then they go back to cooking.

Chin has never had so much beef in his life. As they eat breakfast, wagonloads of soldiers arrive.

"Things are going to be all right now," his father says confidently. "The army is here."

Chin watches the columns of smoke rising from the south and the east. "Henry should be okay. His house is to the west."

His father brushes the fuzz on the crown of Chin's head. "You worry too much."

M R. SMITH COMES back with bad news from the fire station. "They're too busy to come here. People are trapped everywhere. And there are fires all around."

"Then we'll have to do it ourselves," Mr. Travis says. He hands Mr. Smith a bucket.

After another hour of firefighting, the neighbors tiredly plop on the ground.

Henry's arms and back ache. The pails of water are heavy. Wet and sooty, Mr. Travis tells Henry and his mother to take a rest.

Henry watches his father take a turn at the head of the line. He dashes inside the house with the heavy pail.

Water ripples across the pool around the water main.

The ground shakes again. Small waves wash around Henry. Water splashes out of Henry's bucket and over his shoes. Henry waits for it to end. It keeps going on and on.

He falls on the slick cobblestones. He spills the bucket. His mother tries to catch him. But she loses her balance, too.

A wooden house is next to the burning one. It starts to shiver. Boards crack. Splinters fly into the air. The wooden house sags to the side. Glass windows shatter. Inside, furniture thumps against walls. The china plates crash.

"My house," a woman shrieks. She puts her hands to her mouth.

Frightened, Sawyer yips and pulls at the rope around his neck.

"Get out of there," Henry's mother shouts to his father.

Mr. Travis appears in the doorway of the burning house. It is hard to run in the new earthquake. A tongue of fire dances on his shoulder.

The next instant, the wooden house cracks off its foundation. It slides sideways. It smashes into the burning house. Both collapse.

Henry's yell is lost in the roar.

8:15 A.M.
Wednesday, April 18, 1906
San Francisco

AFTER A BIG earthquake, the ground can still shake. It is called an aftershock. The earthquake has weakened many buildings. Aftershocks cause these structures to collapse, too. Even more people become buried in wrecked houses.

The firemen try to rescue the trapped people.

But they also have to put out many fires. Fifty-two fires have been reported. There are probably even more that they have not heard about.

The firemen face many hardships. They have lost their own chief. The earthquake toppled a chimney on him. Others have taken charge.

Some fire companies have also lost their horses. Scared

by the earthquake, the animals bolted from the firehouses. So the firemen pull their wagons by hand. But they cannot travel as fast or as far.

They also don't have enough water. The big water mains have broken in three hundred places. Pipes branch from the water mains into the buildings. There are more than 23,000 breaks in those pipes.

Most hydrants are empty but the firemen do not give up. They find the hydrants that work. They hook up hoses from one wagon to another so they can pump water from several blocks away to a fire. Or they pump salt water from the bay.

But more and more fires flicker into life in the ruins. The flames feed upon broken boards or hissing gas pipes. Soon they swell large enough to swallow entire houses. They are like a pack of wolves attacking where no one expects them to.

Then one fireman remembers an old source of water. Many years ago, water was stored in fifty-seven stone-covered pits called cisterns. Then the city installed water pipes and covered up the old cisterns. Now the firemen break into them.

MR. TRAVIS HAS thrown himself from the doorway. Flames rise from his clothes as he lies in front of the burning house.

Henry is scared. But he is not a coward. He crawls forward over the shaking ground to his father. It is hot by the fire. Steam rises from the wet cobblestones.

"Roll," Henry says and helps his father put out the flames on his fiery clothes. When his father sits up, his hair is curled. The tips are singed.

Once Henry wanted to be like Marshal Earp. Now he wants to be like his father.

The two houses are now one giant hill of rubble. A

bathtub sits upon a section of roof. *Whoosh.* Fire shoots upward. The flames are as tall as Henry's father. Sparks fly like fireflies. They dart onto roofs all around.

"If only the firemen would come," his mother says.

Henry turns in a slow circle. There must be even more fires all around the city. To the south he sees large pillars of smoke. More rise in the east. Chinatown lies that way. Chin lives there. "I think they're even busier now."

Mud and soot streak Mr. Travis's face. He and their other neighbors decide that they cannot rescue their homes. They can only try to save what's inside.

"Our house looks so rickety. Should we really go inside?" Mrs. Travis asks doubtfully.

Mr. Travis takes out his flat wallet and flaps it. "We'll need money. You stay in the street with Henry." He disappears into their house.

Mrs. Travis hesitates. Then she tells Henry to wait for her. She goes inside, too. Henry feels lonely standing there. So he follows his parents into their home. If he helps, they can get out faster.

Henry hears a hiss and looks for snakes. He can't see any in the kitchen. But he can smell gas. The pipe to the stove has broken.

His mother looks at him angrily. But she does not scold him—yet. There is no time. Together, they dump food from the pantry into baskets. They add some dishes, silverware, their pots and a frying pan. Mrs. Travis finds clothes in a hamper. Ah Sing was going to wash them. She takes them now.

Then they stagger to the front door. Mrs. Travis pauses there. She takes six umbrellas from one of the ceramic stands. She hooks them over her forearm and leaves.

Mr. Travis is already outside. He is very mad when they come out. Mrs. Travis nods at the small chest in his arms. "We'll need more than the money in there."

His father grunts that she is right. "But we don't need umbrellas."

Mrs. Travis clutches them. "You never know when they'll come in handy. What if it rains?"

"I hope it does," Mr. Travis says. "It'll put out the fires."

He goes back inside. He changes into regular clothes. Then he comes out with an armload of broken sticks. On his head he wears several of his wife's hats. The top one has a big ostrich feather.

Despite everything, Henry and his mother cannot help laughing. His father looks so silly.

Mr. Travis dumps the wood down in a pile. Then he takes off the feather hat with a flourish. "Madame," he says and presents it to Mrs. Travis. "We don't have a roof anymore. So you'll need this to protect yourself against the sun." He puts his dusty top hat on Henry's head. It hides half of Henry's face until he tilts it back.

His mother holds up a stick of firewood. It is polished, fine-grained wood. "Is this from your mother's Chippendale?" she asks her husband.

"A pile of bricks smashed it," Mr. Travis says with a shrug. Henry knew it was an antique and valuable. It had traveled from England and around South America to reach San Francisco. "We might as well get one more use out of it."

Mrs. Travis goes inside. She changes quickly.

Henry and his father break up thin pieces of veneer for kindling. They are careful not to get splinters. Down the block, the two fallen houses are hidden in flames. The fire is so hot they can feel the heat from where they stand. Henry's father lights their cooking fire with a burning stick from the huge pile.

Mrs. Travis is dressed in regular clothes when she comes out again. She hefts a frying pan from the kitchen utensils they saved. "It won't be as good as Ah Sing's. But it will have to do." As she works, she hums an opera melody.

While his wife is busy cooking, Mr. Travis sneaks back into the house. He drags out his new easy chair.

Other people carry more of their things out of their homes, too. Except for the fires, it is like an outdoor party.

One family has carried out chairs, table and a sofa. They arrange them just as they were inside their parlor. Another has brought out their new bedroom set. After an hour, the street is filled with furniture. A neighbor waves hello from her rocking chair. She sips tea from her best china.

Henry feeds a piece of ham to Sawyer. As his tail wags happily, the Smiths come by. They have piled many things in a baby carriage. "The fire's spreading," Mr. Smith said. A third house is now on fire. "This whole block's going to go up in flames. We're going to my cousin up in Sausalito." That is north across the bay.

"But what if their house is gone, too?" Henry's mother asks.

"We'll keep walking. Eventually we'll find something," Mr. Smith says grimly. "We're done with San Francisco."

"Well, we're not," Henry's father insists.

A cheer goes up from one end of the street. "The army's here."

A squad of soldiers tramps toward them. Henry has never felt happier. He starts yelling. He feels safe now.

However, the soldiers don't stop when people call to them.

As they pass, Mr. Travis says, "Hey, we've got fires to put out and people to rescue."

The sergeant shakes his head. "I'm sorry, but we can't

help you. We're watching for looters."

The soldiers march away. Henry's shoulders sag. The whole street is silent except for the flames.

Mr. Smith grips the handles of the baby carriage. "You're a man of sense, Travis. Save your family. Get out now." He pushes the carriage along again.

Henry jumps when they hear shots. They all turn and look.

"Did the soldiers catch looters?" Henry asks his parents.

"I don't know," his mother says. "But God rest their souls if the soldiers did."

THE EARTH DRAGON IS restless. He tosses and turns on his bed beneath the surface, and more buildings have collapsed in Chinatown. Smoke hangs over Portsmouth Square. Everything looks hazy. Even so, Chin can see new plumes of smoke.

Some of them rise from the direction of Henry's house. He thinks again of the firemen without water.

"We should make sure the Travises are okay," Chin says, worried.

With his son's help, Ah Sing gets up from the grass. He tries a few steps. "I can't walk that far. And you can't go there alone."

"They're probably already leaving on a train," Ah Quon says. "And so should we. The fire is spreading. Think of your boy. Isn't he one of the reasons why you came here?"

Chin's father bites his lip. "I just sent my salary back to China. Can you loan us the money?"

Ah Quon pats his empty pockets. "I'm broke, too."

"A hundred dollars! That's piracy," a man shouts from across the street. A merchant in an expensive robe is arguing with a man on a wagon.

The driver spits on the cobblestones. "Then you can watch your stuff burn or be crushed. There's plenty of others willing to pay."

The merchant pulls at his little goatee. "Okay. But you take me and my family, too."

Ah Quon nudges Ah Sing. "I see our train fares." And he yells to the merchant. "Hey, do you need help loading the wagon?"

The merchant stares at Ah Quon's big arms. "You're hired."

Ah Quon pushes Chin forward. "My partner, too."

"He's too small," the merchant snorts.

"He's small but powerful," Ah Quon insists. "I only work with my partner."

The merchant throws up his arms. "The world is full of pirates." But he gives in.

FIREBOATS AND A NAVY tug join the battle against the fires. They pump salt water from the bay. But in the southern part of San Francisco, many little fires merge into one big fire.

The trouble seems far away from the neighborhood of Hayes Valley. After all, it is near city hall. The firemen are nearby. They are putting out the two small fires.

Everyone else thinks the area is safe. Last night there was a roller-skating carnival at the Mechanics' Pavilion.* A few hours ago, costumed roller skaters played there. Now it

*At the time, *mechanics* meant blue-collar workers.

is an emergency hospital. Injured people cover the floor.

A library has been threatened by the fires in another section of the city. So it has sent 200,000 books to the pavilion. Among them are many priceless manuscripts.

Nearby, a woman's children are hungry. So she starts a fire in her stove. She will cook ham and eggs for them. Flames rise from the wood in the stove. Smoke and sparks rise up the chimney. She cannot see the break in its mortar and bricks. Glowing embers flit from the chimney. They land on the roof. Soon her house is on fire.

To the west, a strong wind races in from the ocean. It sweeps over the rolling sand dunes of western San Francisco. It races through the tombstones of the cemeteries. Stronger than ever, it fans the flames on the woman's house.

The fire swells and swirls. Cinders spread outward like fiery seeds. Most of the fire companies are fighting the flames elsewhere. There are not enough firemen in Hayes Valley to handle this new danger. Soon roofs everywhere are filled with burning flowers. Houses, stores and churches disappear in flame. The firemen are helpless to stop so many new fires. All they can do is retreat. Behind them, they pull their wagons and hoses.

Higher and higher the Ham and Egg fire grows. It rears up like a giant monster. A tongue of flame licks its fiery mouth. It is surrounded by so many unburned buildings. It picks out its next meals.

Then it sees the two other major fires. One is to the south of Market Street. It is chewing on houses and skyscrapers. The other feasts on warehouses in the east.

The Ham and Egg fire stretches one arm east and the other south. It will join its brothers.

S AWYER WHIMPERS at his master's feet. Henry and his parents gaze at the ugly sky. To the south and west a sullen red light hangs above the rooftops. The sky looks like a blue blanket with a crimson border. Smoke rises like black stripes.

Two strangers, a man and a boy, drag a trunk past them. A woman scurries after them. A baby wails in her arms. They look frightened.

"Do you want something to eat?" Mrs. Travis calls to them. "We have more than enough."

They do not pause to stop. "San Francisco's on fire. Get out now!" The man waves north toward the bay. The sky there is still mostly blue.

"This is our home," Mr. Travis says stubbornly.

"Wait," Mrs. Travis says. She wraps the baby in her expensive shawl. "She could catch cold."

As the people leave, Mr. Travis hugs his wife. "I've never loved you more." And Henry has never been prouder of his mother.

Minutes later, three men pull a two-wheeled cart piled high with belongings. An old woman perches on top of the furniture. She is weeping and wailing. "We're doomed," she keeps crying. A boy trails them leading a dazed woman by the hand. She stumbles along.

More people pass by. Many pull heavy trunks. Others drag their possessions along on blankets.

A young man holding a wedding cake staggers by. Next to him is a woman wearing so many layers of clothing that she can barely walk.

Henry thinks, "People save the oddest things."

Some pull carts or wheelbarrows or even toy wagons. Others use anything with wheels. They push cribs, beds, lawn mowers, sewing machine tables or upright pianos along the street. On them, they pile everything they can.

The trickle of people grows into a stream. Then it becomes a river.

The smoke grows thicker across the rooftops. Houses are burning all around them. The flames peer hungrily down at Henry. Burning embers drift in the hot winds like angry butterflies. Some hiss as they land on the wet cobblestones. Others start small fires. Henry can see threads of smoke rising from their house.

Mrs. Travis snaps open an umbrella. She puts it over her head. "Maybe this will protect us from the sparks." Her husband and son do the same.

It is so hot now that the moisture rises in steam from the street. The avenue is filled with people who resemble ghostly snakes. Even their clothes feel warm to the touch.

An ember lands upon Mrs. Travis's umbrella and burns through the fine silk. She gives a cry when it lands on her sleeve. Mr. Travis puts it out with his hand. Sawyer gives a sharp bark of pain. Henry brushes an ember away from his pet's fur. His hand stings now. He wants to comfort the little dog, but he is too scared.

As flames tower in the sky, Henry stares silently at the fire.

EVEN WHEN the Earth Dragon lies still, Chin cannot forget he is angry. Fire has transformed the whole sky into a sullen red banner. The smoke makes Chin cough. Soot mixes with his sweat and stings his eyes. His face becomes striped like a tiger's.

The merchant works him and Ah Quon hard. Ah Sing tries to help them but he cannot do much. The merchant shoos him away. "I don't pay for a crippled pirate, too."

"You don't have to pay me," Ah Sing says. But Chin and Ah Quon make him sit down.

After that, Chin keeps an eye on his father. He makes

sure he rests. "Why can't he just relax?" he grumbles to Ah Quon.

"Because your father's not comfortable doing nothing," Ah Quon grunts. "He's a brave man."

Chin remembers when they were buried. "He told me to save myself," Chin says.

"It sounds like him," Ah Quon says. "But I wasn't talking about the earthquake. Your father came to a new country. And he's worked so hard. He's spent so many years away from his family. That takes real courage."

Chin had not thought about that. "There are all kinds of heroes."

The driver finally tells the merchant that his wagon cannot carry any more. The merchant protests that he is not done yet.

Ah Sing calls to the merchant and points to the Fire Alarm Station. It is a small brick building on the other side of an alley on the west side of Portsmouth Square. "The firemen are leaving." He waves at the Hall of Justice. "The police and officials and soldiers are going, too."

The merchant slaps his sides helplessly. Then he shouts to his family. "Let's go." He settles up with Chin and Ah Quon.

A small boy and girl totter out of the house. They are dressed in expensive silk. Their faces are clean. They stare at Chin's grimy face as if he is some strange beast.

"Don't touch that filthy boy," the merchant's wife scolds them. She is wearing fancy clothes and all her jewelry. She glitters like the Travises' chandelier. Some ash lands on her expensive silk robe, leaving a black spot. "My best robe is ruined," she complains.

She and her family need Chin and Ah Quon's help to climb up on the wagon. Their hands leave sooty marks. The merchant's wife is almost crying. She tries to clean off their handprints.

"Could you give my friend and his son a ride?" Ah Quon asks the merchant.

"Only if you leave some boxes behind," the driver says. Of course, the merchant refuses.

The horse can barely pull the load down the street.

Ah Quon lifts his head. He whinnies like a horse. Then he squats down. "Hop on, neighbor. I'll be your mount."

Ah Sing climbs onto his friend's broad back. "What's the price?" he teases.

"More than you can afford," Ah Quon says and stands up.

They start south. The Earth Dragon has destroyed far more downtown than in Chinatown. But the street is blocked by fallen buildings. They detour to the east. That block is already burning. The firemen and soldiers try their best, but there is no more water in the cisterns.

They use knapsacks, blankets and even brooms to beat out small flames. They clear spaces with axes and shovels. That way there is nothing to burn. To Chin, they seem like mice nibbling at a fiery monster.

The heat is too intense. Chin, Ah Sing and Ah Quon have to make detour after detour.

"This is like a maze," Ah Sing says.

They reach Market Street at last. They stop there. The south side is a giant wall of flame. Some of the skyscrapers are already just steel skeletons. Their collapsed walls burn at their base like a garden of red and yellow flowers. Others are ablaze. They look like giant torches. Chunks of flaming buildings crash to the sidewalk. Specks of soot and fiery sparks fill the air. They look like hordes of angry flies.

"We can't get to the trains," Ah Quon says in dismay. He coughs from the smoke.

The southern flames have cut off many others. Chin watches the panicked people stumble east along Market Street.

Ah Sing points and says, "They must be going to the ferries."

"Then so are we," Ah Quon says. With Ah Sing on his back, he breaks into a trot. Chin runs by his side.

Automobile drivers desperately toot their horns. Drivers on wagons crack their whips. People are too frightened to step aside. Soon all the vehicles are stuck.

Ah Sing, Ah Quon and Chin dodge around all the obstacles. They always keep moving.

There is so much smoke now. It is hard to breathe. The fire roars in their ears. The heat makes them sweat. It is like being in a furnace. What if the fires have reached the ferries? Then they will be trapped.

People begin to drop their belongings. Chin and his father and Ah Quon stumble over hats, bags, boxes and trunks.

Suddenly people scream in horror. Chin turns and looks over his shoulder. A furry gray carpet sweeps toward them. Thousands of rats are trying to escape the fire, too. They brush Chin's ankles as they scamper past.

At last they see the ferry building. It towers through the haze. It looks ready to fall at any moment. But the flames have not reached it yet. Chin hopes the Earth Dragon will stay quiet until they pass through it to the ferries.

The waterfront is filled with all kinds of ships. There are small ones and big ones. There are steamships and sailboats. There are passenger ships. There are also fishing boats. They stink from their loads. There are even a couple of Chinese ships called junks.

Tugboats toot as if telling everyone to hurry. On some of them the sailors shout out the fare. They want a lot of money. Ah Sing would have to work months for the amount.

"There are the real pirates," Ah Sing says.

Chin is worried. Do they have enough for the ferry?

A huge mob surrounds them. It carries them forward toward the ferry building.

Everyone is fighting to escape the fire. Men shove women and children and elderly people out of their way. They knock over injured people on crutches or in stretchers. Several have guns. They point them at anyone in their path.

The gate goes up. The mob pours onto the ferry. Automobiles and wagons are abandoned. The sailors make people leave their trunks and luggage and boxes. They are dumped on a growing pile.

"Grab hold of my shirt," Ah Quon says to Chin.

Chin clutches the hem. Ah Quon charges forward. They shove past the carts. They squeeze between wagons and automobiles. Ah Quon is like a runaway bull.

Then an automobile tries to lurch out of line. It bumps Ah Quon. He drops Ah Sing.

"Save yourself, boy," Ah Sing commands Chin.

The crowd surges around them. Their feet will trample Chin's father and friend.

Chin swallows. He is terrified. But he remembers his

father and the bull. He has to be just as brave.

"I'm not leaving without you," Chin says.

He stands over them. He shoves, elbows, punches and even bites. But he gives them time to stand back up. "That was very stupid," his father says. He leans on Chin. "But also very brave. Thank you."

Bruised, they stagger forward. The crowd sweeps them over the ramp and into the crowded ferry.

No one takes their money. Today the ferry is free.

The boat rides low in the water. It is carrying too much weight. The sailors are afraid the boat will sink. They shove people back onto the pier. "There'll be another boat soon," they promise. Then they cast off the lines. The big side wheels churn the water white.

Many people are left behind. They beg and cry and offer money.

One man with a suitcase leaps from the pier. But he misses the boat. He is hauled back onto the land.

The passengers are all silent. San Francisco has changed so much. All its tall buildings have fallen or are on fire.

The overloaded ferry chugs across the choppy green water. A sheet of flame covers the ruins. It slithers across San Francisco like a dragon with red spines.

Chin says a prayer for Henry.

2:30 P.M.
Wednesday, April 18, 1906
San Francisco

THREE HUGE FIRES burn in San Francisco. One swallows up the south. The other sweeps toward Chinatown in the east. But the Ham and Egg fire is the worst. It swallows whole city blocks. It grows fatter than its brothers.

The firemen try to stop it, but it is too big and there are too few of them. They have little water. The fire sweeps around them.

It swallows up the ruins of city hall. Before it devours the gigantic Mechanics' Pavilion, the patients are taken out in time. But the books and manuscripts stored there are all lost. The wisdom of ages turns to ashes.

All the firemen can do is retreat again.

THE FLAMES FORM walls on three sides now. The air becomes hotter and hotter. Ash and embers swirl all around them.

"We have to go," Mrs. Travis insists.

There are tears in Mr. Travis's eyes. He takes one last look at their house and then nods. "You're right."

Mrs. Travis bites her lip. "We could save more if we only had a cart or a wagon."

Henry sees the ladder by the Smiths' house. Then he thinks of his new skates. "We can make our own. We can tie the ladder to my roller skates. They're in my room."

His mother shakes her head. "The stairs are too rickety."

"I'm light," Henry points out.

"Absolutely not," his father says.

His parents search for something with wheels. Henry waits. When their backs are turned, he runs into the house. It creaks around him. He can smell gas. Still he goes to the stairs. It tilts to the side.

He goes up. The first step groans under him. It wobbles precariously.

"Henry, come back here!" his mother calls.

He can hear his father coming for him.

It is now or never. Henry dashes up the stairs. Each tread moans in protest under his feet. Then the whole staircase begins to shake. He holds on tight to the railing.

"Come down here this instant!" his father demands from the bottom of the stairs.

"You're going to spank me anyway. So I might as well come down with the skates," Henry insists.

He starts to climb again. The stairs wobble back and forth. He slips near the top but is able to crawl onto the second floor.

Everything is jumbled together in his room. Henry throws books and toys around. The remaining walls look as shaky as the stairs. Finally he finds his skates.

He races back into the hallway. His father looks up at him, worried. Mr. Travis tries to support the staircase. "Hurry!"

Henry grips the railing again. He stumbles down the steps. They sway like a boat deck in a storm.

His mother grabs him from the bottom step. "You are a very, very bad boy," she scolds. "But I'm very proud of you." She draws him outside.

His father quickly lashes the skates to the ladder. They pile all they can on it. They take along pots, a frying pan, dishes, silverware, food and clothes. They will have to leave most of their belongings behind.

"I should have gotten blankets instead of this. But this will have to do." Mr. Travis adds his grandmother's lace tablecloth to the pile.

Mrs. Travis holds up her umbrellas. "We can't leave these behind."

"They'll just add to the weight," Mr. Travis complains.

"We'll need these," Mrs. Travis insists. "I feel it in my bones."

Mr. Travis grumbles, but he adds the umbrellas.

As a last precaution, Henry wraps a rope around his waist. Then he ties the other end to Sawyer's collar.

The smoke shuts out the sky. In the haze, the sun looks like a bright ruby. Mrs. Travis's flowers in the window boxes glow like coral.

Mr. Travis pulls their makeshift cart with a rope. Mrs. Travis and Henry push from behind. The last of their neighbors are deserting their homes, too.

They walk to a big unburned street. A river of people flows north, away from the relentless flames.

The street is jammed. The Travises cannot move fast. The ladder is hard to steer, too. Then someone's cart breaks down. Everyone moves around it. Desperately, its owners try to fix it.

Sawyer has trouble walking. His legs are too short. So Henry slings him around his shoulders.

They pass by sandlots full of tired people sitting like statues upon their trunks and boxes. They are too weary to move. However, they refuse to abandon their belongings. They simply watch as the fire comes toward them.

Mr. Travis shouts at them to leave.

They ignore him.

Other people begin to lighten their loads. They drop clothes, frying pans, pillows, even couches and chairs. The litter becomes an obstacle course.

The Travises have to dodge around them. Behind them the fire grows. Above it, black smoke fans outward like hair.

Suddenly the street explodes. Cobblestones whiz everywhere. People scream. Mr. Travis falls.

Flames burn upward from the new hole.

Mr. Travis sits up. His arm is bruised. "I smell gas," he says. "The earthquake must have broken the gas main."

He gets up. They start forward again.

Boom! Boom! Boom! More spots blow up. More stones fly through the air.

They duck and keep moving on.

The east is hidden in smoke and flame.

Henry hopes Chin has gotten away in time.

3:00 P.M. to 4:00 P.M.
Wednesday, April 18, 1906
San Francisco

 OST OF THE cisterns are empty now. The fire wagons cannot pump enough water from the bay to stop the three big fires.

Creating a firebreak is one way to battle a fire. A big space is cleared. With nothing to burn, the flames stop.

In a few places that morning, the firemen have already used dynamite to create firebreaks. They blew up whole buildings. The flames could not spread across the rubble.

Now the firemen make a desperate decision. They will dynamite everywhere. But soon near Chinatown they run out of dynamite and have to switch to black gunpowder instead.

But the firemen are not sure how much powder to use. They put too much in a burning building on the eastern side of Chinatown. The explosion sends flaming fragments high in the air. They rain down all over Chinatown. Fires quickly sprout up on a dozen roofs. A dozen becomes two dozen. And then three.

In no time, all of Chinatown is blazing.

Again, the firemen pull back.

8:00 P.M.
Wednesday, April 18, 1906
North San Francisco

 HE TRAVISES HAVE fled to the northern edge of San Francisco. The waters of the bay roll by, cold and swift.

They squeeze into a field with everyone else. Nearby, Fort Mason is full of soldiers.

Next to them a big man sings a song in German to his wife and daughter. His little concertina looks like a toy in his huge hands. On their left, a Mexican family makes dinner by a campfire. The mother makes tortillas on a flat rock. Henry has never heard so many languages. The whole world seems to have camped here.

Some have brought tents. Others make them out of sticks and blankets.

Mr. Travis makes a tent out of one umbrella and the tablecloth. He jams the shaft into the dirt and opens the top. Then he spreads the tablecloth over it. The fine lace is like a giant spiderweb.

"I told you the umbrellas would come in handy," Mrs. Travis says.

Mr. Travis winks at his son. Then he teases his wife. "All right. Maybe they were useful just this once."

It is almost like a gigantic picnic. But there is no safe water for Henry. The only water is in the bay. It is too salty to drink. There is plenty of liquor. But Henry cannot touch it. Some adults do and they get very noisy.

Soon everyone grows silent. Flames fringe the hilltops. Smoke towers over them. It is like a giant black worm. It swallows the moon and the stars.

Henry hugs Sawyer. His pet licks the soot from his face.

Nearby, a man holds up a picture of Saint Francis toward the flames. San Francisco was named after that saint. The man's thick black beard twitches on his chin as he prays loudly in Italian.

The fire seems like a living monster now. It has taken their homes. Now it wants them. It reaches out fiery paws.

But they can run no farther. The bay is behind them. No one knows what to do. They watch the fire creep toward them.

T HE EASTERN FIRE sweeps through Chinatown toward Nob Hill.

And stops.

Firemen and soldiers and volunteers make a stand on the steep slope of Nob Hill.

Like a hungry beast, the eastern fire eyes the fancy hotels and mansions there. It reaches for them again and again. Each time, the firemen force it back.

Downtown, firemen and soldiers hold back the Ham and Egg fire as well. They protect the big hotels and stores.

Then a fire starts in a downtown theater. It could be careless soldiers who lit it. It could be someone who hates the owner. No one knows.

Soon sparks fly everywhere.

The firemen downtown are caught between the theater fire and the Ham and Egg fire. Frantically they roll up their hoses. Then they pull their wagons down fiery canyons.

The wind fans the flames of the Ham and Egg fire. It grows higher and stronger, sweeping like a wave over downtown. It races up Nob Hill toward the other firemen.

The Nob Hill defenders will be trapped. The eastern fire is in front of them. The Ham and Egg fire is coming from the side. They leave, too.

With a roar of triumph, the eastern fire surges up Nob Hill.

Mansions and hotels sit helpless. Their huge windows shatter from the heat. Expensive wallpaper and paintings blacken and burst into flame. Costly rugs shrivel and burn. Fancy brass doorknobs melt. Fragile glassware shatters. Antique furniture and silverware become blackened lumps. Huge crystal chandeliers crash from burning ceilings.

On top of Nob Hill, the Ham and Egg fire and eastern fire merge. They become one giant monster now.

It is the firemen's worst nightmare.

CHIN AND AH SING'S cousin, Ah Bing, buys fish from fishermen. Then he sells the catch to stores and restaurants. His warehouse is at the Oakland waterfront. He welcomes Chin and Ah Sing. "I thought you were dead."

"Almost," Ah Sing says.

They go out to the pier and stare at the blazing city.

Fire covers San Francisco's hills, changing night to an eerie twilight. It colors the billowing clouds of smoke a brick red. It reflects off the bay waters like a flight of scarlet arrows.

Ah Quon is with them. He brushes some ash from his

sleeve. "No one's alive in that," he says.

The Earth Dragon has taken a terrible revenge.

"Poor Henry," Chin says.

"Poor everyone," his father says.

Noon
Thursday, April 19, 1906
North San Francisco

F LAMES FILL THE sky. Clouds of smoke roll overhead like copper waves. At noon it is only a sullen twilight.

The heat and the ash make it hard to breathe. Soot covers everything. Lost dogs and cats prowl all around.

Henry holds on to Sawyer tight. They are still at the northern edge of San Francisco. His thirsty pet wants to drink from the salty bay. Henry is tempted himself. His mouth is parched. The water rolls by so close.

No one sings or plays instruments anymore. Everybody is too scared. They huddle together. Some stare. Some weep. Some pray.

They all listen.

Boom! Boom! Boom!

The firemen and soldiers are still blowing up buildings and creating firebreaks. The flames keep coming anyway.

Mr. Travis coughs. "I want you to know one thing. I love you both very much."

Mrs. Travis hugs him and Henry. "And we love you."

Henry feels like crying, but the tears don't come. He is too dry inside.

All of a sudden, people begin to scream in terror.

"Runaway horse!" someone yells in the distance.

The horse is a big beast. It usually pulls heavy wagons. At that moment, it is free. Its hooves thunder as it gallops. Its eyes are wide with fear. A broken tethering strap dangles from its harness. People jump to either side. The panicky horse cuts through the crowd like a ship through a sea.

Henry holds Sawyer tight and gets up.

The little German girl next to him just sits and stares. She is too terrified to move. Henry stumbles over her.

Desperately Mrs. Travis picks up a pink parasol. She opens and closes it. She yells at the top of her lungs. Mr. Travis grabs a red umbrella and flaps it, too. He shouts as well.

The bright shapes of the umbrellas swell and shrink fast, startling the horse. It stops and rears up. Its hooves flash in the air. Mr. Travis drops the umbrella and darts in.

The horse sets its forelegs down for a moment. Mr. Travis grabs its bridle. He has timed it perfectly.

Their Mexican and German neighbors help him hold the horse.

Mr. Travis speaks soothing words. The huge horse trembles but listens and stays still.

Mrs. Travis folds her parasol in triumph. "What did I tell you about the umbrellas?"

Mr. Travis bows. "I will never laugh at your collection again," he promises.

Afternoon
Thursday, April 19, 1906, to the afternoon of Friday, April 20, 1906
San Francisco

THE THREE MAJOR fires fuse into one titanic monster.

They become the Great Fire.

The Great Fire sprawls over most of the city. It devours wood. It curls steel beams like hair.

It sucks the air from all around it, casting off more heat than a thousand furnaces.

A big blaze like the Great Fire creates a firestorm. A fire heats the air. Then the hot air rises. Cold air rushes in and takes the place of the hot air. With small fires, it is just a draft. With the Great Fire, it is giant gusts of wind. They fan the flames, making them even bigger. The winds can knock people and animals back into the fire itself.

Water boils at 100 degrees Celsius. The air in the Great Fire is twenty times hotter than that.

At such a high temperature, wood and cloth and flesh burst instantly into flame. Most metals will melt.

The Great Fire is huge. So is its appetite. It sweeps on like a tidal wave over the hills. Buildings ignite at its touch.

More navy ships sail into the bay. The crews can see the Great Fire. They dock anyway at the unburned piers. From the ships, brave sailors and marines march into the city.

San Francisco will not give up.

Van Ness Avenue is a broad street. It is perfect for a fire-break. Many of the firemen gather here to make a stand. They dynamite the mansions on either side. Huge clouds of dust mix with the smoke.

The houses they set fire to burn down quickly. The Great Fire will find nothing to feed on.

The army sends its cannon. Big horses clop down Van Ness. The gunners jump down from the limbers and unhitch their guns. They aim them at the fancy houses and fire. Shells shatter glass and splinter wood. They pound the mansions into ruins. It is a real war now.

The Great Fire halts at the firebreak on Van Ness. Hungrily it reaches for the unburned houses beyond. But the area is too wide. Only sparks land on the other side of the firebreak. Firemen quickly fling buckets of water on them.

A navy tug pumps salt water from the bay. It travels in a miles-long hose to the firemen.

They also find two hydrants that still work. They hook up more hoses to these. Then they shoot streams of water against the flames.

The Great Fire tries to sweep north of the firebreak, where mansions still stand.

The dynamiters and gunners race ahead of the Great Fire to extend the firebreak. Firemen dash into buildings and place their dynamite. Then they set the fuse and run out. Sometimes they have hardly left the mansion before it explodes. The army gunners fire their cannon yards away from their targets. Firemen and gunners dodge the flying debris and move on. They must keep ahead of the hungry flames.

The firemen hold most of Van Ness Avenue. But then the Great Fire slips south. It gets ahead of the firemen. Flames claim the still erect mansions on one side of Van Ness. From these rooftops the Great Fire sends flaming darts across the street. Soon the mansions are burning on the other side.

The Great Fire crosses Van Ness Avenue in that spot. It

has won the race. The rest of the city lies helpless before it.

Firemen and gunners must coax scared horses back into their harnesses. Then tired men and animals stumble one block west to Franklin Street.

They will make a new stand there. The desperate battle begins again.

The Great Fire forces them back another block to Gough Street.

The firemen start over. They will not give up.

SAN FRANCISCO is still burning. Flames cover the hills. Most of the buildings are gone. But there doesn't seem to be as much smoke.

Ah Quon and Chin heft crates of fish onto a wagon. Ah Sing checks a list. He says, "People still have to eat. And we have to work."

They are the lucky ones. Fifty thousand people have fled to Oakland. They live in tents set up for them. But Americans object to living next to Chinese. So Chinese survivors have to live in special camps.

Chin glances back at San Francisco. Will the Earth Dragon strike again? So many people have died. He hopes Henry isn't one of them. Every time a ferry comes in, he scans the crowd for his friend.

He does not pay attention when a navy ship docks at another pier. He does not know that the navy is now carrying people to safety.

He is still working when he hears, "Chin! Ah Sing!"

It is the Travises. Their clothes are singed. They look dazed like the other passengers. Sawyer is in Henry's arms. The dog barks a greeting.

Chin jumps down from the wagon. He is about to hug Henry but stops.

"What's wrong?" Henry asks.

"I stink of fish," Chin says.

"I smell of smoke," Henry laughs. They hug anyway. Sawyer licks their faces.

Ah Sing greets the Travises. "Can I help you with your luggage?"

"The ship would take only us," Mr. Travis explains.

Mrs. Travis holds up her umbrellas. "But I refused to lose these."

Mr. Travis winks. "You scared those poor sailors. You looked ready to hit them with the umbrellas."

"And I would have, too," Mrs. Travis says. She brandishes her umbrellas like swords.

Ah Quon is resting on the wagon bed. Chin introduces him now. Ah Quon nods.

"Do you have someplace to stay?" Ah Sing asks the Travises.

"I have a cousin in Sacramento," Mrs. Travis says.

Mr. Travis makes a face. "He's a big windbag. I'm staying in San Francisco."

"Where?" Mrs. Travis asks.

Mr. Travis waves a hand at the burning city. "We'll build it bigger and better."

"And where do we stay in the meantime?" Mrs. Travis demands.

Ah Sing clears his throat. "It's a little smelly, but I could ask my cousin, Ah Bing."

So the Travises move in with Ah Sing and Chin's cousin. It's a good thing they like fish.

5:00 P.M.

Friday, April 20, 1906, to 7:00 A.M., Saturday, April 21, 1906

San Francisco

THE FIREMEN STILL have not given up. By the late afternoon, they have gathered all around the edges of the Great Fire. They are making their last stand. If they do not stop it now, there will be no city left.

In sandlots and parks, the survivors huddle under blankets. Embers and chunks of burning wood rain down on them.

The firemen make new firebreaks. Bravely they dart into buildings and blow them up.

On Telegraph Hill, people pick up sacks. They tear curtains from windows. They soak the sacks and curtains with water from an old well. When the water runs out, they use wine. Desperately they beat back the flames.

The army cannons boom again. Between the smoke of the fire and their gunpowder, the gunners can barely see.

One of the gunners is almost blinded by the fire, but he refuses to leave when the doctor tries to make him go to a safer place. He is the only one with experience on that gun crew. The others wheel the gun to the next spot. They carry him there. Despite the pain, he opens his eyes. He aims the gun. The force of the explosion knocks him down. The others move the gun on. Then they lift him up and bring him there. He does it over again.

On the waterfront, the navy ships pump water into hoses. Sailors and firemen direct the nozzles at the flames.

Inland, firemen and volunteers form bucket brigades. They use anything that can hold water, from buckets to big milk cans. Other firemen climb up to the roofs. When the shingles catch fire, they use axes to chop away the pieces and throw them off. Sometimes they even use their bare hands.

Behind them, others wait with blankets, sheets, brooms, mops, burlap sacks and coats. They rush in and beat out any embers or burning wood.

People even tear doors from houses for a pair of firemen

to hold like shields. Behind the doors, a third person uses a blanket to smother the flames before they can start new fires.

The doors blacken and smolder from the intense heat. The teams can work for only a minute or two. Then they must retreat from the smoke and heat.

New teams pick up the doors. They advance again to continue the fight.

Again and again the Great Fire tries to expand. Again and again the firemen drive it back.

In one spot, invisible, poisonous gases build inside the Great Fire. It spreads the gas over the firemen and knocks them out.

Everywhere, the fierce heat starts melting the firemen's rubber coats. They throw themselves into the gutters or puddles. Then they roll around to cool off their clothes.

By now, all the firemen are exhausted. They gasp for breath in the hot, hot air. The heat makes some of them faint. Brave volunteers dart in and drag them to safety. Then they take their place.

The desperate struggle goes on for hour after hour. Firemen, soldiers, sailors and volunteers refuse to give up.

Early Saturday morning, three days after the Earth Dragon woke, the Great Fire hesitates. Then it stops. Then it pulls back. Now it is the Great Fire's turn to retreat.

With new hope, the firemen drive it back foot by foot. Coughing in the hot, smoky air, they press on relentlessly. Their charred boots slosh through the wet ash and mud.

Everywhere the Great Fire withdraws before the determined people. Block by block it is forced back through the smoldering ruins. It clings hungrily to the burned timbers. But there is nothing left to eat. The flames begin to wither. Slowly, ever so slowly, they shrink.

The firemen and volunteers have won!

AH SING, AH QUON and Chin have been working all day. They look across the bay at San Francisco every now and then. Black clouds still rise from the city, but there are only a few fires left.

Then a ferry brings the news. The Great Fire is dying.

In the early evening, they go to the pier with the Travises. They can see the ruins more clearly.

Everything hits Chin now. They have lost their homes and all they own. Worse, they have lost their friends in Chinatown and the cable-car men.

Silently he begins to cry. He glances at Henry. He is crying, too. All of them are crying. Even Ah Quon. They have not had time to feel sad until this moment. They have all been too busy trying to survive.

Then Chin feels something wet touch his cheek. At first, he thinks it is a tear. But then he feels another and another. His shirt is wet. He looks up. It is raining.

Henry puts out a hand. "Too bad it couldn't have come sooner."

"At least we have umbrellas," Mrs. Travis says. She shares them around.

Mr. Travis opens his. Then he winks. "They are *very* handy."

Late afternoon
Sunday, April 29, 1906
San Francisco

By Saturday, April 21, twenty thousand people have fled San Francisco by boat. Some 225,000 have left on the trains.* The trains and boats take them all over California.

But others are stubborn like the Travises. They want to rebuild their homes. The Travises are eager to return to San Francisco. "I can swing a hammer with anyone," Mr. Travis says. He makes a muscle.

His bank has reopened though it is just a tent and a

*Never have so many people left an American city in peacetime— until Hurricane Katrina struck New Orleans.

small iron vault. He could commute from Oakland on the ferry, but he decided to camp out in the tents that have been set up in Golden Gate Park.

Eleven days after the earthquake, Ah Sing borrows his cousin's wagon to take the Travises to the park. After the Travises rebuild their house, Ah Sing will work for them again. Chin will go to school. But it will probably be in Chinatown. If there still is a Chinatown.

Henry doesn't think it's fair that Ah Sing and Chin cannot stay with them. The Chinese are not allowed in the park. They are being moved to Oakland and other cities.

"The people in San Francisco don't want to let us go back to our old neighborhood," Ah Sing sighs. "They want us to build a new Chinatown in Hunter's Point."

"If you Chinese own your land, that won't happen," Mr. Travis says. "You tell your friends to see me. I'll give them the names of good lawyers."

Ah Sing guides the wagon off the ferry. They go through the dark tunnel of the ferry building. They pull out of the traffic and stare.

The Great Earthquake and Fire have left nothing. There are just hills of rubble where buildings had been. Here and there a steel beam curls upward like a burned pretzel. A charred wall marks where a store once stood. Ribbons of smoke rise everywhere. Everything is still smoldering. Mud and ash cover the cobblestones.

"It's like the moon," Mr. Travis says eventually.

Then they hear a clink. Three men are going through the rubble. One of them picks up a brick. "This one is still good." He adds it to a small pile.

"You see," Mr. Travis says with new confidence. "People can't wait to start over." He can already see buildings and not ruins.

The next moment Sawyer leaps off the wagon. Henry and Chin jump after him. The little dog scampers over the rubble excitedly. After a long chase, Henry scoops his pet up.

"We don't have time for this," Henry scolds him. Then he notices a bit of color in the dust. "What's this?" He picks it up. It is a cheap paper book. Someone must have dropped it. It survived somehow. On the cover is a cowboy. He blazes away with his pistols.

"It's one of those penny dreadfuls." Mrs. Travis frowns.

"Let them keep it. It may take the boys' minds off things," suggests Mr. Travis.

A few days ago, they used to read books just like that one. Life seemed so dull then.

Chin shakes his head. "You keep it, Henry. I've had enough excitement." He hopes that the Earth Dragon will sleep a good long time.

Henry looks at their parents sitting on the wagon. They aren't dismayed by the wreckage. They're ready to rebuild their city. That takes more courage than capturing outlaws. He whispers to Chin, "And we don't have to look far for heroes. They were right under our noses all this time."

Henry tosses the book to the side. Then he climbs on the wagon with Chin and Sawyer.

They'll have enough adventures building a new city, too.

AFTERWORD

The U.S. Army lists 672 people dead or missing in San Francisco and the surrounding area. But the United States Geological Survey estimates the number should be three or even four times higher. Historian and San Francisco City Archivist Gladys Hansen believes the death toll is above 3,400. Officially, only twelve Chinese died. But the Chinese handled their own dead after the Great Earthquake and Fire. They shipped the bodies back to China for burial. So the real number will never be known.

The Great Earthquake and Fire destroyed more than 28,000 houses, stores and other buildings. Between 2,381 and 2,593 acres became a wasteland. The losses were about $400 million in damage by 1906 standards. But dollars were worth more then. Fourteen dollars could comfortably feed four people for a week. Groceries cost a lot more nowadays. So do houses. The damage in 1906 would cost the equivalent of over $7 billion dollars in 2000.

Most people think the fire was more destructive than the earthquake. That may not be true.

Historian Gladys Hansen has done a great deal of research. She found a report from an army captain that stated some people deliberately set fire to buildings wrecked by the earthquake. They did that because their insurance covered damage from fires but not from earthquakes. Then they told the insurance companies that the fire had ruined them.

That was fraud.

The investigators from the insurance companies said that the Great Fire damaged the buildings. Even so, the insurance companies refused to pay their customers. This made it hard on the people who had told the truth, and they sued. In the end, the insurance companies paid only a small amount to everyone.

After the earthquake, the railroad companies were afraid they would lose money if people stayed away from California. So they also told everyone that the Great Fire had caused most of the damage. People can defend against fires. It is harder to protect against earthquakes.

No one will know for sure how many buildings were actually wrecked by the earthquake or by the fires. Once the Great Fire swept over the ruins, it became impossible to tell.

Despite the massive destruction, San Francisco carried on. The city buried its dead, cleared the debris and rebuilt itself. At first, survivors lived in tent cities scattered around San Francisco. Later, the tents were replaced by shacks. Life was hard in these camps. Before the earthquake, about

400,000 people lived in San Francisco. After the earth-quake, the population decreased to about 175,000.

Recovery was even more difficult for the Chinese. Some fled the city. Those who tried to stay had a lot of trouble. Wherever they went, some white citizens would object, and the Chinese would then have to move to another spot. By May 6, only 186 Chinese were living in a single camp in the Presidio. The others had left or had been moved to camps in Oakland.

The city tried to keep the Chinese from returning to the site of their old homes. However, the Chinese asserted their property rights. White landlords also wanted their Chinese tenants back. In the end, Chinatown was rebuilt on its old location.

For many years, San Francisco was filled with the sound of hammers and saws. It smelled of raw wood and new paint.

Just nine years after the earthquake, the city held the Panama-Pacific International Exhibition. It celebrated the opening of the Panama Canal. It also showed the world that San Francisco had recovered. People came from around the world to see it. Among them was Laura Ingalls Wilder, who was covering the event for her local newspaper. The Palace of Fine Arts, still standing today, hints at the scale and loveliness of the exhibition's buildings.

As I mentioned in the preface, Chin, Henry, their families and friends are imaginary. However, the details about the earthquake and fires are based on facts. Animals were nervous before the earthquake. Afterward, horses and cattle stampeded. And a panicked bull was shot in Portsmouth Square by a policeman. After the earthquake, people saved the oddest things. That included a wedding cake. At least two Chinese junks took away passengers. In the refugee camp near Fort Mason, an Italian man held up a picture of Saint Francis. People also stopped a runaway horse by flapping umbrellas at it.

My description of the night before the earthquake is also based on facts. Enrico Caruso sang in an opera. There was also a roller-skating carnival. The best costume really did win $1000.

I have personal connections to the earthquake as well. Like Ah Sing, my grandfather was a houseboy. He had gone home to visit his family in China. He returned to America on April 19, 1906. In those days, Chinese landed at the pier of the Pacific Mail Steamship Line. They were then kept in a building. Immigration officials would question them there.

However, on Thursday, April 19, the Great Fire threatened the entire waterfront. My grandfather probably landed on Angel Island instead, where he was detained until April 26. It would have been his first encounter with Angel Island. He would come to know it well. In later years, immigrants arrived there from China. One of them was my father.

I have also experienced many earthquakes in San Francisco. On March 22, 1957, an earthquake hit the city that registered 5.3 on the Richter scale. It was enough to shake our school. I wrote a science fiction story based on that memory. It was the first story I ever sold.

Then, on October 17, 1989, another big earthquake hit. That measured 7.1 on the Richter scale and caused a lot of damage. My wife, Joanne Ryder, and I knew how bad it was from listening to our battery-powered radio. However, we couldn't see the wreckage because we had no electricity, so our television didn't work. The next day Joanne had to fly to a conference. Somehow we made it to the airport. A few airplanes were still leaving. When she got to the conference, she could see the destruction on television. Unfortunately, our telephone had gone dead by then, so she couldn't reach me. I was fine, but she was very worried.

In recent years, scientists have reexamined the 1906 earthquake. They have inspected the rocks in the fault lines again. They have gone over the written records. They are debating the strength of the 1906 earthquake. Some now think it measured between 7.7 and 7.9 on the Richter scale.

Every year San Francisco honors the dead on April 18. People gather to remember that day. A hydrant at the corner of Twentieth Street and Church provided water that saved part of San Francisco. On the anniversary, it is given a fresh coat of gold paint.

Every year San Francisco and other cities train for a big earthquake. Firefighters and police prepare for emergencies. Buildings are constructed better and stronger.

We know that one day, another big earthquake will come. We do not know when or where.

We only know the Earth Dragon will wake again some day.

Selected Reading:

The most accurate information on the San Francisco Earthquake can be found in Gladys Hansen and Emmet Condon's book, *Denial of Disaster*, San Francisco: Cameron and Company, 1989.

For the revision of the death toll numbers, please see:

Herel, Suzanne. "1906 Quake Toll Disputed: Supervisors Asked to Recognize Higher Number Who Perished." *San Francisco Chronicle*, January 15, 2005, B1.

Other books to read are:

Barker, Malcolm E., ed. *Three Fearful Days: San Francisco Memoirs of the 1906 Earthquake and Fire.* San Francisco: Londonborn Publications, 1998.

Bronson, William. *The Earth Shook, the Sky Burned.* Garden City, NY: Doubleday & Co., 1959.

Coxe, Mabel. Letter to her brother, C. C. Coxe. Reprinted in the *San Francisco Chronicle,* April 13, 1997.

Lowe, Pardee. *Father and Glorious Descendant.* Boston: Little, Brown, 1943.

Mack, Gerstle. *1906.* San Francisco: Chronicle Books, 1981.

Thomas, Gordon, and Max Morgan Witts. *The San Francisco Earthquake.* New York: Stein and Day, 1971.

Wong, H. K. *Gum Sahn Yun.* San Francisco: Fong Brothers, 1987.

There are a lot of websites on the Internet about the San Francisco Earthquake and Fire. Two of the most reliable websites belong to the United States Geological Survey (USGS):

quake.wr.usgs.gov/info/1906/

and the City of San Francisco Museum:

www.sfmuseum.org

On Sacramento Street on Nob Hill, looking east toward Chinatown and the advancing flames. Note the building on the right that has lost its front like the Smiths' home. The Travises lived below the western side of Nob Hill.

The earthquake wrecked these houses on Golden Gate Avenue near Hyde, close to the city hall and Hayes Valley. On his way to the ferry, Chin would have passed to the east of these.

A chimney fell through the roof into this bedroom, but the owner—like Henry's parents—was fortunate not to be in it.

Photo of the fire in the downtown area, taken from Powell Street near Sacramento Street on the eastern border of Chinatown.

In the area that the firemen, soldiers, sailors and volunteers had saved, people camped out with what they could salvage. This is a camp in Jefferson Square at Eddy and Turk, near where I later grew up.

The Travises, Chin and his father would have seen these ruins in the downtown area when they returned.